TILLY'S PONY TAILS

Samson
the stallion

D1516460

TILLY'S PONY TAILS

Samson
the stallion

PIPPA FUNNELL

Illustrated by Jennifer Miles

Orion
Children's Books

First published in Great Britain in 2009
by Orion Children's Books
a division of the Orion Publishing Group Ltd
Orion House
5 Upper St Martin's Lane
London WC2H 9EA
An Hachette UK Company

3 5 7 9 10 8 6 4 2

Text copyright © Pippa Funnell 2009
Illustrations copyright © Jennifer Miles 2009

The right of Pippa Funnell and Jennifer Miles to be identified
as the author and illustrator of this work has been asserted.

The Orion Publishing Group's policy is to use papers that are natural,
renewable and recyclable products and made from wood grown in
sustainable forests. The logging and manufacturing processes are
expected to conform to the environmental regulations of the country
of origin.

A catalogue record for this book is available from the British Library.

ISBN 978 1 84255 712 9

www.orionbooks.co.uk
www.tillysponytails.co.uk

For my god daughter,
Georgia Brown

One

It was a chilly winter's day but Tilly Redbrow didn't mind what the weather was like – rain, wind, sleet or snow. As long as she got to ride and spend time with the horses at Silver Shoe Farm, she was happy. Tilly was horse mad, and now that she shared her own pony, Rosie, with her friend, Mia, there was always an opportunity to ride, groom, feed, clean or simply be

around the animals she loved. Tilly had taken on Rosie after Cally, the third member of their pony-mad gang, had gone to boarding school.

Today Tilly was particularly excited about her weekly riding lesson because Angela, her instructor, had suggested she was ready to start jumping. Over the months, Tilly had worked hard trying to perfect the basics of walk, trot and canter. She had very good natural balance and the ponies instantly responded to her aids.

Tilly was excited, and a little bit nervous. After years of dreaming it felt great to be actually doing it.

Angela had laid a few poles on the ground and placed several cross poles around the arena.

"The idea," Angela explained, as Tilly led Rosie into the enclosed area, "is that these exercises over the poles and cross poles will help you learn to judge your stride, maintain a rhythm and assist you with keeping straight. At this stage it's not about how high you can jump, it's about

perfecting the basics to boost you and your pony's confidence."

Tilly gulped.

"Don't look so worried, Tilly – you're ready for this!"

Tilly studied the challenge in front of her. The poles were very low, and she had watched her friends, Mia and Cally, jump much bigger obstacles hundreds of times before. It would be fine, she told herself.

"Before you tackle it with Rosie, try walking it yourself, so you can get a sense of the distance up to the jump. Four of your strides is about equal to one horse stride. Then allow two of your strides for the distance from the fence to where she's going to land, and two more in front of the next fence for where she'll take off. If you watch at the shows and events, you'll see all the riders do this to judge how many strides there will be between fences. Even top class riders do it."

Tilly handed Rosie's reins to Angela, and walked over to the cross pole. She paced around, thinking very hard about where she would have to take off in order to clear it. She walked round one more time, checking the height, and then returned to Rosie.

"I'm ready," she said.

"I'll help you mount then," said Angela, offering her a leg up.

Riding Rosie always felt good. There was very little that upset her, and Mia said she had a natural impulsion to get herself over any obstacle in front of her. Tilly knew it wasn't like that with every horse. She remembered how she'd struggled with Bunny, the pony she had learned to ride on, whom she'd had to kick endlessly because she was so lazy.

Of course, the one horse Tilly really wanted to jump was Magic Spirit. He was the reason she had come to Silver Shoe

Farm in the first place, so he held a special place in her heart. Ever since Tilly had helped Angela rescue him from a busy roadside, the bond between them had grown and strengthened. And even though she had an affinity with all the horses at the farm, he was her number one.

As Tilly thought of him, while warming up Rosie, she briefly touched her horsehair bracelets: one contained tail hairs from Magic, and the other she'd had since she was adopted as a baby. The feel of them made her more confident, and she concentrated hard on what Angela was saying.

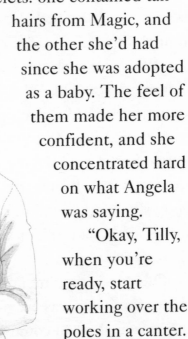

"Okay, Tilly, when you're ready, start working over the poles in a canter.

I want you to concentrate on maintaining a constant rhythm."

Using Angela's measuring system, Tilly guessed that the poles were placed around five horse strides apart.

"You should meet both poles on an even stride – and by that I mean Rosie should not have to suddenly take a great long stride just before the poles, or a very short one. That's it," Angela said encouragingly. "Heels firmly down. Relax your knees."

It took several goes before Tilly got the hang of it, and when she was doing the exercise smoothly and consistently, Angela said she was ready to move on to the cross poles.

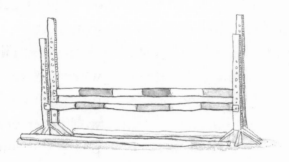

"Now I want you to do exactly the same over the first cross pole as you've just done. Keep very straight, then jump it in the middle," called Angela.

Feeling nervous, Tilly immediately grabbed the reins more tightly, and her whole body tensed.

Rosie, sensing Tilly's unease, quickened her pace at the cross, met it on an awkward stride, but jumped it nevertheless. And though Tilly was delighted to have left the ground for the first time, she felt annoyed with herself. She had done everything Angela had told her not to do!

"Don't worry, Tilly, try again!" said Angela. "The more you practise, the better you'll get."

When Tilly had successfully jumped the first cross and met it on the correct stride, Angela suggested she try two in a row, aiming for four strides between each.

Confident now, Tilly met the first cross perfectly but then, excited by her success, she forgot to sit up straight on landing. As

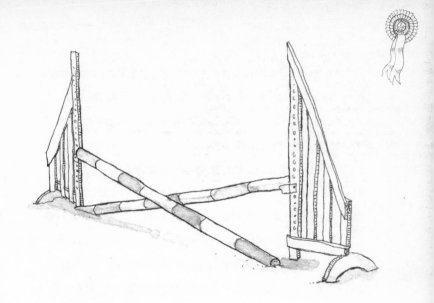

she approached the second cross, she realised too late that she was perched too far forward and so Rosie added in a stride on take off.

Disaster!

As soon as Rosie was in the air, Tilly felt her upper body thrust forward. She lost her balance, and fell from the saddle as soon as they landed.

"Ow!" she cried, tumbling on to her front. Luckily, Rosie seemed to know just what to do and stepped aside safely.

Angela ran forward.

"Tilly! Are you okay?"

It felt as though someone had punched her in the ribs. She sat up slowly, and gasped for air. Angela crouched beside her, using her first-aid skills to check Tilly over.

"I think you've winded yourself a little bit, Tilly. Don't worry, there's no lasting damage. But maybe you should take it easy for the rest of the day."

"But what about the cross pole?" cried Tilly, determined. "I didn't make it. I want to have another go. I know what I did wrong ... I didn't keep my legs secure for the second jump ... I forgot about my balance ... this time I'll get it right..."

"There's plenty of time for you to try it again," soothed Angela. "Let's just make sure you're okay first. We'll get you a drink in the club room."

Tilly sighed and with Angela's help, gradually stood up.

"Did it look really messy?" she asked, embarrassed by her disastrous jump.

"Well, it wasn't the neatest attempt in the world, but I tell you what, I did exactly the same thing when I tried my first jump."

"And you fell off?"

"I sure did! Still got the scar to prove it."

Angela lifted her sleeve, and showed Tilly her arm. There was a three-inch mark down the middle of it.

"Broken in two places!"

"Ew!" said Tilly.

"But as soon as I was ready, I got straight back on, and I know you will too, Tilly. You're like me – determined."

Two

Angela took Tilly to the club
room and made her a cup of
hot chocolate. As Tilly sat
down on one of the comfy
armchairs, she noticed a large
cardboard box lying beside it.

"What's in there?" she
asked.

"Oh, they're the Silver
Shoe Farm Christmas
decorations," explained Angela. "I've been

meaning to put them up around the club room, but I haven't found the time yet."

"I'll do it!" said Tilly eagerly.

"Great," said Angela. "And here comes one of your little helpers..."

Just then, Mia burst into the room, moaning about the cold.

"It's fr-fr-fr-freezing out there! Feel my fingers."

She whipped off her riding gloves and rubbed her hands against Tilly's face. Tilly winced.

"They're like ice blocks!"

"Here, have a hot chocolate," said Angela, passing Mia a warm mug. "Perhaps you can help Tilly with the Christmas

decorations once you've warmed up a bit.
I've got to go and check the post and take a
look at Magic on my way."

The girls sipped their drinks and
discussed Tilly's tumble at the
jump. Mia reassured her that
she and Cally had fallen from
Rosie many times – but always
got back on.
Then they set to work
with the tinsel and
baubles.
When the box was
empty, and shiny
decorations were draped
and dangling from every possible piece of
furniture, the girls sat back and admired
the effect.

"It looks like the inside of
a tin of sweets!" laughed Mia.

"It's nice, but it's not very
... horsey," Tilly pondered.
"We need to give it the
Silver Shoe touch."

"I've got an idea!" said Mia. She pulled out a box of stationery and a pile of old magazines from beneath the table. There were copies of *Pony*, *Horse and Hound* and *Equestrian Life*.

"Look through these and find good pictures," she instructed.

The girls leafed through the magazines. Tilly found it hard not to get distracted by the facts and stories in them.

"That one's perfect," Mia said eventually, pointing to a photo of a handsome palomino. She tore it out, and added a flurry of tissue snowflakes to the background. Then she cut a Santa hat from a leftover Christmas card and glued it to the palomino's head.

"There you go – he looks much more festive now!"

Together, they made several more festive pony pictures,

adding glitter and snowmen and reindeer antlers; then they stuck them on the walls around the club room.

A little while later, Angela returned, with a pile of letters and leaflets in her hand. She looked harassed, but took the trouble to admire the girls' decorating efforts.

"Very nice! From now on, you can decorate every year. Right," she said, sighing. "I've got good news and bad news."

"Tell us the good news first," said Mia.

Angela held out a letter.

"We've managed to get tickets for the Olympia Horse Show this year, so we're going to organise a coach trip. If you want to come, sign up here."

Tilly clapped her hands together. She had wanted to go to Olympia ever since she was tiny.

"It's the best thing ever!" cooed Mia. "I went last year. The horses are incredible! They perform a Christmas

pantomime and everything! You'll come, won't you?"

Tilly nodded, wide-eyed. As if she'd miss it!

"They have some of the top show jumpers in the world, and the Mounted Police do a display, and at the end of every performance Father Christmas appears, all the little kids in the audience get really excited – it's so much fun!"

Mia talked so quickly, Tilly could hardly keep up with her. Both of them were so excited they forgot that Angela had said there was some bad news as well – until Tilly noticed an uneasy look on her face.

"What's wrong, Angela?"

"I've just been down to the stable block," she said slowly. "I had a long chat with Duncan. I'm afraid there's a problem with Magic Spirit."

Tilly's face dropped. In that instant, all her excitement melted away.

"Wh-what is it?" she asked quietly.

"Well, it might be nothing, but he's showing signs of colic. He's sweating a lot and kicking at his tummy. He's obviously got some abdominal pain. With that sort of thing we can't take any chances, so the vet is on his way."

Tilly shuddered. Angela squeezed her shoulder.

"Can I see him?" she whispered.

"I think he'd like that. You'll give him more comfort and reassurance than anyone. Why don't you and I go there now?"

Three

Magic Spirit was in his stable. As soon as
Tilly saw him she felt a rush of emotion.
He looked so sad and uncomfortable. His
eyes, which normally had a bright twinkle,
were half-closed. Usually, whenever Magic
saw Tilly, he would buzz with excitement
and come straight towards her. Today, he
just lurked at the back of his stable, staring
at her from the darkness.

They heard a car pulling up in the yard.

"That must be the vet," said Angela.

"I'll go and get him."

Tilly entered Magic Spirit's stable and went to comfort him.

"Oh, Magic," she said soothingly. "You poor thing. Don't worry. We're all here to look after you. I'll do my best to make you feel better."

Magic lifted his head slightly and rested it on her shoulder, as though anything else was too much effort. Tilly stroked his neck with one hand while rubbing his nose with the other. As she did, she thought as hard as she could about him feeling better, feeling

strong and powerful again, galloping across
a prairie with her on his back. She
desperately hoped these good thoughts
would help him.

Angela and Brian the vet came into the
stable. Tilly recognised him, as he was
often at the farm, doing health checks and
vaccinations. Recently he'd been busy
looking after Lulabelle, one of the young
mares, who was pregnant with her first foal.
But it wasn't often that he had to come to
look after a sick horse. Silver Shoe Farm
worked hard to keep their animals healthy.

"So here's Magic Spirit, eh?" said the
vet, placing his medical bag on the floor
beside him. "I must say, he's come on well.
I remember doing a check up on him when
he first arrived – he was so thin his ribs
were poking out. Now look at him – he
looks like a serious performer."

Tilly and Angela were encouraged by
his words. Despite his illness, it was
obvious Magic was an impressive horse.
Thanks to Tilly's special care and everyone

else at Silver Shoe Farm, he now looked powerful and well-nourished. His true potential was starting to shine through.

"We've been breaking him in," said Tilly proudly. "Duncan says I might be able to ride him soon."

"Good stuff," said the vet, smiling at Tilly. "Now, let's see what the matter is, shall we?"

The vet approached Magic Spirit and said hello, then he returned to his bag and pulled out a selection of instruments. Tilly and Angela stood silently watching. Tilly knew that the vet was there to help, but the sight of all his equipment made her feel nervous.

"I'll check his vitals, then I'll examine his abdomen. From what you've said, it sounds like tummy trouble."

The vet took Magic Spirit's pulse and temperature, and checked his breathing. As he did, he asked Angela questions.

"How long has he been like this?"

"It came on really suddenly. Duncan

noticed he was behaving oddly, trying to
rub his belly and sweating. So we called
you straightaway. Yesterday he was okay."

"Well, his temperature's definitely up,"
said the vet, sounding serious.

Tilly tensed. Angela curled an arm over
her shoulders to reassure her.

The vet took his stethoscope and started
moving it around Magic Spirit's belly, so
that he could listen to the rumblings of his
digestive system.

"I can't bear it," whispered
Tilly anxiously. "He'll be
okay, won't he?"

"I hope so," said
Angela. "But
colic is one
of those
things,
Tilly.

Horses can't burp or be sick like we can, so whatever they ingest has to work its way through their system. If they eat something poisonous or pick up a bug, it can cause big problems. Brian knows what he's doing though. I tell you what, let's go and get him a cup of tea, and then when we come back, he'll be able to tell us what's happening."

Brian looked up and smiled, as though he also thought a cup of tea was a good idea. So Tilly kissed Magic Spirit on the forehead, then followed Angela back to the club room. While she was there, she phoned her mum and dad, and asked if she could stay at the farm a bit later than normal – she had to make sure Magic Spirit was going to be all right before she went home.

To take her mind off things, Angela showed Tilly the leaflets for the Olympia Show. It looked brilliant.

"Maybe you and your mum can come," she said. "A weekend in London – when you're not at the show you can get some Christmas shopping done."

"Yeah," said Tilly, picturing a massive stadium full of top horses. Although she knew her

mum would be more interested in the shopping part.

"I'll book some space for the two of you."

By the time they got back to the stables, the vet had finished his examinations. He was peeling off his medical gloves. Magic was lying down, looking very sorry for himself.

"Unfortunately, as I suspected, Magic has a blockage in his intestine," he explained. "I've pumped liquid paraffin into his stomach via a tube through his nostrils – he didn't like it very much, but fingers crossed it will do the trick."

33

Angela looked grave. This made Tilly worry, even though Brian was being positive.

"What now?" she asked.

"Well, the next twenty-four hours are critical. As the oil works its way through, it should ease the blockage, and then that will be that. What we don't want, is for it to become an intestinal catastrophe."

Tilly knew what that meant. She closed her eyes and gulped. She'd read about it – a twisted intestine could mean surgery or, worse, that the horse had to be put down. Her hands started to tremble so she gripped hold of her horsehair bracelets and tried to steady herself. She wore two side by side now – the one she'd worn all her life, woven from black tail hairs and fastened with a silver clasp, and another special one that her mum had woven from tail hairs that Tilly had collected from Magic Spirit's tail. It had been

34

a surprise extra birthday present and Tilly wouldn't be parted from it.

"Keep him as calm as possible. Hopefully he'll lie still for the rest of the night. I'll be back to check on his progress in the morning. If you're worried about anything, just give me a call."

Angela thanked Brian and went outside with him. Meanwhile, Tilly lay down next to Magic and put her arms around his neck.

Tears rolled down her cheeks and dripped on to his coat. They were tears of sadness, but also tears of relief, because at least she knew there was a good chance he would be okay. She had to stay strong for him.

Four

The following day, Tilly visited Magic
Spirit, and then every day the next week,
before and after school. She didn't mind
the early starts in the cold and dark. And
she didn't complain about having to get
through a long day at school, before going
to Silver Shoe Farm, and then getting
home and *still* having to do her homework.
Magic came first.

Sometimes, she took magazines and
books and sat reading to him. His

favourites were *Black Beauty* and *National Velvet*. At least once a day, she groomed his coat because he found it relaxing. She told him about things she'd been doing at school, and asked him questions about homework she didn't understand. He stared at her quizzically – occasionally looking as though he was trying to think of an answer. But Tilly knew he was probably just daydreaming about bags of carrots and oats and sugar lumps.

Over the days he seemed to improve, although he was still weak and unsteady on his feet. The good news was that the blockage in his intestine had eased. Early on Saturday morning, the vet came to check on him. He could see the sparkle was returning to Magic's eyes.

"It would be good for Magic Spirit to go out to pasture now, to get some air and fresh grass. I'm delighted he's made a recovery. To be honest, I wasn't sure, you know. Horses in his state haven't always pulled through."

"I think Tilly's nursing has been a big help," said Angela. "She's looked after him every day and made sure he's stayed calm and relaxed."

"Well, it's definitely made a difference," the vet said, smiling, as he reached into his medical bag.

"There you go," Angela said quietly, nudging Tilly's shoulder. "I know you said you wanted to run your own stables when you grow up, but maybe you should consider becoming a vet?"

Tilly pondered this, then she reached up and stroked Magic's face.

"What do *you* think?" she asked. "Do you think I'd make a good vet?"

Magic pricked his ears and snorted.

"That's a yes!" said the vet, and everyone laughed.

Now that Magic Spirit was on the mend, Tilly was able to think about other things. Especially the Christmas trip to the Olympia Horse Show. She heard adverts for it on the radio and couldn't believe that in only a matter of weeks she would be going to watch it herself. It was her favourite topic of conversation at breakfast, lunch and teatime.

"I want to see everything," she explained to her mum. "All the top class show jumping, and the military horses, and the pantomime, and the bit when Father Christmas arrives. And I want to look around all of the trade stands..."

"Phew!" sighed her mum. "Sounds like we'll be busy!"

She passed Tilly a bowl of her special homemade muesli. It had cranberries in it, to add festive flavour. Tilly thought they were delicious. Adam, her little brother, didn't, and kept picking them out and flicking them on to the floor.

"Please don't do that, Adam," said Mrs Redbrow.

"It's okay, Mum," he said. "Scruff's eating them. He's like a hoover!"

Scruff was the Redbrow family's long-haired terrier. Sure enough, he was gobbling up all the cranberries on the floor. Tilly chased him away.

"I don't think they're good for a dog's diet," she said. After her worries with Magic Spirit, she didn't want to take any chances.

"What do *you* know?" sneered Adam.

"More than you, freak boy! I might be a vet one day! So there!"

Adam poked out his tongue and Mrs Redbrow rolled her eyes, as if to say: Too early for silly squabbling.

"I've got so much to do," she grumbled. "I haven't even started the Christmas shopping yet."

"You can do it when we go to London," suggested Tilly brightly. "They've got all the big stores there. We can go to Oxford Street, and Covent Garden, and then we can go to Buckingham Palace and see the mounted guards . . ."

"Somehow," said her mum, with a dry smile, "I can't imagine we'll be doing anything other than looking at horses!

There probably won't be much time to get to the shops."

"Well, as long as they sell riding gear, I won't mind going in a few."

"I don't need to ask what *you* want for Christmas this year then!" said her mum, smiling.

Five

The morning they went to Olympia, Tilly and her mum had to get up very early. Their alarm clocks went at five o'clock. For Tilly, this wasn't a problem because she'd already been lying awake for half an hour, imagining how good it would be to parade Magic

45

Spirit in the Olympia arena, in front of all those spectators.

"Next we have the crowd's favourite, Magic Spirit. Look at that horse's configuration!"

She could hear the commentator's voice in her head:

"What a beauty, and an interesting story too. His owner, Miss Tiger Lily Redbrow, rescued him from a roadside when he was just four years old. She used her extraordinary skills to nurse him back to health, and turn him into

the fantastic ride he is today. He's one of the top horses in the country, worth hundreds of thousands of pounds, but she'll never sell him. In fact, rumour has it, he won't allow anybody to ride him but her..."

"Tilly!"

The words of the commentator were replaced by the sound of her mum's voice, whispering through a crack in the door.

"*Tilly*! Are you awake yet? We've got to get going. The coach will be here soon."

Tilly climbed out of bed and splashed water on her face. She had hoped she would be able to squeeze in a visit to Silver Shoe Farm beforehand, so she could be certain Magic was feeling okay, but her mum said there wasn't time.

She'd seen him the previous evening, and knew that he was enjoying being out in the long field. He was keeping himself to himself, not too keen on socialising with the other horses – except for his companion, Lina, the miniature skewbald Shetland – but that was quite normal for Magic. It was a relief to know

she was leaving him in a healthy state, but
it was hard to imagine two whole days
without seeing him.

Tilly and her mum waited for the coach
by the front gate. Tilly wore skinny jeans,
a long stripy scarf, and her warmest fleece.
As she sat on the wall, she looked through
the pictures of Magic she had stored on her

mobile, and wondered what it would be like if horses could use mobiles. That way, it would be easy to check up on him!

The coach pulled up outside Tilly's house just after five-thirty. It was good to get out of the cold winter air. Mia and her mum had already got on and were sitting near the back. When the two girls saw each other they waved excitedly, but there were too many people on board for them to sit next to each other. Instead Tilly and her mum took a seat near the front.

"Right. Let me sort my bits out. I've got a bag of wine gums, some cartons of juice, magazines, puzzle books – would you like anything?" said Mrs Redbrow, as she rummaged through her bag and got comfortable

"I'll be all right," said Tilly, knowing she had music on her mobile and plenty of daydreams to keep herself entertained.

Mile by mile the journey sped away. It was still dark outside and the roads were quiet. Tilly hoped they would get to London in good time. The quicker they got there, the more time they would have at Olympia.

Once the sun had risen and they were rolling down the motorway, everything looked the same distant towns and endless fields. Tilly stared from the window and tried to spot the perfect location for her dream stables. It should be a long way from the motorway, she decided, near plenty of fields and some forest. Maybe near a river too, so the horses could go down and refresh themselves on summer evenings.

"Wh-where are we?" said her mum, confused and groggy. She had fallen asleep as soon as they'd left Cosford.

"Er, somewhere called Luton," explained Tilly, checking the road signs. "Is that near London?"

"Not far – we'll probably be there within the hour."

Tilly felt a thrill ripple through her.

She tried to make the time go faster by
counting how many horse trailers they
passed. By the time they pulled off the
motorway, she'd spotted three small ones
being towed and one of those lorries that

could carry at least six horses. She tried to catch a glimpse of the driver, to see if it was anyone famous, but they passed too quickly.

At last, the coach burrowed its way into the busy streets of London. The traffic slowed, and although Tilly could tell they were close to the exhibition hall, it seemed as though it was taking forever to get there.

"It wouldn't be like this if everyone was on horses," she mumbled, stuffing a couple of wine gums into her mouth.

Much to Tilly's frustration, once they arrived there was still more delay. They

had to check into their hotel, which was only round the corner, and then Tilly's mum wanted a cup of coffee. They sat on comfy armchairs in the lobby, and Mrs Redbrow commented on the stylish furnishings while Tilly fidgeted.

Eventually Mia and her mum came down.

"Hey. What time are you going to the show?" asked Mia.

"Now!" said Tilly.

"Soon!" said her mum, at the same time.

"Let's all go together then," said Mia's mum.

Six

Fortunately the queues for Olympia were
not too long. They already had their tickets,
which they had to present at the turnstile
and then, at last, to Tilly's joy, they were in!

The entrance area was bustling with
people. In the corner was a massive
Christmas tree, dressed with multicoloured
baubles as big as footballs. A group of carol
singers was standing beside it, performing
'Jingle Bells'.

"Ooo!" said Mia, squeezing Tilly's arm.

"I *love* this time of year! Let's look at the trade stands and see if we can find a Christmas present for Rosie."

"Good plan," said Tilly.

They had an hour before the show started, so they headed to the shopping village. The variety was overwhelming. There were shops selling every piece of riding equipment the girls could ever need, and probably stuff they didn't need. There were clothes, boots, wet-weather gear, riding hats and helmets, crops and whips, grooming kits, pony accessories,

such as ribbons and blankets, and all kinds of saddles, reins, bits and stirrups. Some of the stalls advertised different types of feed or miracle cures for common horse health problems. Others were promoting riding centres and training grounds.

"It's pony paradise!" gasped Tilly, unable to take it all in.

They browsed the pony accessory stalls and, after some debate, agreed on a cute gingham winter blanket for Rosie. But Tilly didn't forget Magic Spirit either – she found

him a gorgeous, soft sheepskin numnah. He deserved something cosy to wear under his saddle after everything he'd been through. And maybe soon, Tilly would get to ride him while he was wearing it.

As they were making their way towards the main arena, Tilly spotted something she'd wanted for ages – the latest crash helmet. Angela had recommended this one, particularly now she was learning to jump. It would be perfect, but she knew it was too expensive and she'd already spent her money on Rosie and Magic.

Tilly's mum caught her eye and reached for her purse. Then she said with a wink, "Pay me back when you've made your fortune as a top international three day eventer!"

There was just enough time to grab sandwiches and smoothies for lunch, which they ate sitting on the steps near one of the entrances to the main arena. As they munched, they heard a ripple of applause coming from inside.

"What's going on in there?" asked Mia. "We might be missing something."

"I thought the show didn't start till one," said her mum, checking the programme of events.

Tilly stood up and peered through the doorway.

"Are there any horses out there yet?" asked Mia impatiently.

"Not horses," said Tilly, shaking her head. "Dogs!"

"Oh, it must be the Kennel Club Dog Agility performance – they're on before the main show begins."

"Aah!" cooed Tilly and Mia together. "Let's go and watch!"

And before their mums could protest, they were dashing through the entrance and scrambling to their seats.

"But what about your sandwich? Oh, *never mind*!" said Tilly's mum.

The dogs were fun to watch, but the real excitement began when the main performance was announced and people started to take their seats. In the arena, stewards were scampering about, putting out fences and setting up obstacles for the first show jumping class. Tilly, Mia and their mums were sitting at the side, not too far from the front row. They could see everything clearly.

"I'm seat number 77J," said Tilly. "Seven's my lucky number!"

"What's first?" asked Mia.

"It's the Christmas Cracker Speed Stakes."

Tilly soon found out that this was a thrilling jumping class against the clock. It was won by a jockey called Mark Slater and his horse Troy, one of the up and coming British talents.

Next came the Shetland Pony Grand National.

The music started and everyone cheered. A group of charming Shetlands were led into the middle of the arena to massive applause. They paraded in front of the judges, just like Red Admiral had done at his race meeting. Then their young riders mounted and were led to the start.

"They're just like miniature versions of proper Grand National riders!" said Mia. "Even their silks look the same. They're so sweet."

But there was nothing sweet about the race itself. It was fast and frenetic. The riders and ponies threw themselves over the fences, all determined to be first to the finishing post. The girls were impressed.

The next event was a display by the Mounted Metropolitan Police. Tilly wasn't sure what to expect from this, but when the loud dance music, flashing lights and smoke machines started, she realised it was going to be something special. She slid to the edge of her seat and gazed at the spectacle.

The horses emerged from a bright halo of white light and gathered in a ring. As the music got faster, their movements got faster, until they were galloping in a circle. The crowd loved it and clapped along in time to the beat.

"This is incredible!" said Tilly.

The horses carried out a series of jumps, at a very fast pace and in perfect synchrony. None of them seemed at all bothered by the loud noises and flashing lights.

"How do they get them to do that?" said Mia. "Even the bravest of the horses at Silver Shoe Farm would freak out if all that was going on around them!"

"They're police horses, aren't they?" said Tilly. She'd read about it in the programme. "They have to be trained to cope with all sorts of scary things, in case they have to work during riots and stuff."

"Fire!" gasped Mia suddenly.

Several large upright hoops had been set ablaze in the middle of the arena.

One by one, the horses took turns to leap through the flaming hoops. They were as casual about it as they would be if they were jumping over cross poles in Jack Fisher's field. It was exhilarating to watch.

"They're the bravest horses I've ever seen," said Tilly admiringly, as the crowd got to their feet and cheered.

While the next event was being set up, one of the officials announced a competition to win a backstage tour of the Olympia arena. It was hard to hear exactly what he was saying, but it seemed as though he was reading out numbers.

"Imagine that," said Tilly. "Going behind the scenes would be brilliant. You could see the horses close up, and there might be some famous people back there!"

"Dream on," said Mia. "We never win anything!"

Every time the announcer called out a number, someone, somewhere in the audience would stand up and cheer.

"It's like a raffle," said Tilly's mum. "If he reads out their seat number, they've won a tour."

The girls carried on chatting non-stop, wondering who would win the next jumping class – the Puissance. It was the first event after the interval, and was all about which horse could jump the highest wall. Tilly and Mia also talked about the Grand Finale. This year it had a Scottish theme.

"The best bit is when Father Christmas appears on his sleigh!" said Mia.

Suddenly they were bathed in light. A spotlight was on them. They both blinked towards it.

"Number 77J! Our final winner of the backstage tour is the lucky person in seat

number 77J!" came a voice over the loudspeaker.

"77J? That's my number," said Tilly, bewildered. Then she realised. "That's me! I've won!"

She stood up and clasped her hands to her mouth. She couldn't believe it. Mia and their mums smiled and clapped.

Once Tilly had calmed down a bit, her mum explained.

"The tour takes place during the interval. You'll have to meet the group at the main entrance in a bit."

"How cool!" said Tilly.

She sat back and tried to enjoy the rest of the first half, but her mind was elsewhere, wondering what she'd see and who she'd get to talk to when she went behind the scenes.

Seven

Tilly felt very privileged as she and her mum made their way down to the meeting point.

"Enjoy it – and make sure you get back to your seat in time for Father Christmas!" said Mia, waving them off.

There were so many people around and, of all of them, Tilly felt she was the luckiest.

"There they are," she whispered, catching sight of the official tour guide. He was surrounded by eager, happy faces, and was wearing a silver steward's badge and a uniform so that everyone could identify him.

They introduced themselves to the official. He explained that everyone should stay close to him; there was a lot going on backstage and he didn't want anyone to get hurt. Tilly kissed her mum goodbye and went to stand with the rest of the group. Her knees kept jiggling because she was so excited.

Fifteen other people were waiting with her. Tilly glanced about her. There were women and men of all ages but it looked as if she was the youngest. She noticed a couple of girls, probably about sixteen or seventeen, standing together but not making conversation. One was wearing a smart quilted jacket and designer jeans. The other was scruffier, wearing a checked shirt, denim skirt and cowboy boots.

"Okay, ladies and gentlemen," said the official. "My name's William, but you can call me Will. We're about to go through the doors and into the collecting ring area. Again, I ask you to stay together at all times. That way we can keep everyone safe and get you back in time for the rest of the afternoon show. Is everyone enjoying themselves?"

There was a big chorus of 'yes'.

"Let's go then. Feel free to ask any questions."

They shuffled into formation behind Will, and went through a doorway where a pair of strict-looking security guards stepped aside. Will turned to everyone and said,

"You're very honoured – the public don't normally get to see this bit!"

They emerged into an area where lots of people were gathered at a long bar area. It was carpeted and there were a number of tables around. Tilly thought this must be a special area for the riders, owners and grooms to get something to eat and drink.

After walking through this area, they came to some sand, and now Tilly saw the collecting ring. She was shocked at how small a warm-up area it was, but as Will quickly pointed out, they were in the middle of London, and they did have to fit everything – including stables – into this small space.

"As you'll probably have guessed, this is the collecting ring," said Will. "It's where the horses warm up before they perform. Then they gather in the small area over there where their grooms and riders can watch closed circuit television screens which show them what's happening in the main arena. Through those large doors is the arena itself – if you stepped through it now, you'd have the entire audience staring at you! Can you imagine how exciting it gets in here before one of the big classes?"

Tilly pictured a scene of nervous, twitchy horses, all desperate to show off their skills. She imagined the Metropolitan Police steeds getting ready to gallop out in formation and then jump through their fire rings. But imagining them was all very well – when would she actually get to see one?

As the collecting ring was relatively quiet, Will led everyone up the right-hand side of the warm-up area. Tilly beamed as she saw a row of eight small heads popping out of their tiny stables. She recognised the Shetland ponies from the Shetland Grand National. Their jockeys had clearly got into the Christmas spirit because the stables were decorated with tinsel, streamers and paper chains.

Then they came to some bigger horses. "These are the carriage horses that will appear in the finale," explained Will. "All the horses and ponies on this side are involved in the displays. Now if we go back to the other side of the collecting ring, you'll see that's where all the international show jumping horses are."

Will told them that the Show Jumpers had to be kept separately from the rest of the horses, and under the protection of even more security guards.

"But where are the police horses?" asked Tilly, looking around. She was thinking about what she'd read in the programme.

"I'll show you them next," replied Will. "There's not enough room for twenty police horses here, so they're in a small hall just beyond the Jumpers."

The tour moved on and stopped outside a row of vast tack rooms. Tilly had never seen so much equipment all in one place before. There

were racks of bridles, bits, reins and saddles that went from the floor to the ceiling.

The smell of leather dressing was divine! Everywhere she looked there were stable hands. She assumed they must be in the police force because they were all dressed in navy blue with a Metropolitan

Police badge on their jumpers. They were all scrubbing, brushing, waxing, and polishing – making sure everything was clean and shining. When they saw the tour they looked up and smiled, but they were too busy to stop working.

"It's a lot of hard work," said Will.

Tilly didn't mind the idea of hard work. She wished she could be one of the stable staff. To her, it looked like a wonderful job.

As they walked back into the original hall, they passed the Stable Manager's office.

"Ted, our Stable Manager, is responsible for everything that happens backstage," explained Will. "As you can imagine, it's a hard job keeping everyone happy and the show running smoothly!

"And now for the Show Jumpers!" he said, leading them past yet another security guard.

Ahead of them, a magnificent grey was being led down the corridor by his groom, with his rider walking alongside. Tilly recognised Mark Slater, the winner of the first class, and his horse, Troy. She twitched with excitement. She could see why the horse was so agile and quick over his fences. He was enormous. He made her pony, Rosie, look like one of the Shetlands!

Mesmerised by his powerful conformation, she admired the horse for a while. Eventually Troy was led out of sight, but by the time Tilly stopped staring at him, she realised the tour group had got ahead of her. At the end of the aisle between the stables she could just see the top of Will's head bobbing about. She was about to chase after him when a sudden bang startled her. The bang was followed by a loud whinny. It felt so close it made her jump. She glanced around and realised it was coming from the stall behind her.

It was a sound she understood, because it reminded her of what Magic Spirit had been like when he'd first arrived at Silver Shoe Farm. It was the sound of distress! Without hesitating, Tilly leaned up over the door and looked inside.

Eight

At first, the horse didn't notice Tilly. He threw his head back and continued to whinny and kick at the sides of his stable with a hind leg. He kicked at the door and tried to rear, but because of his size he ended up knocking into the walls of the stable. It was as if he was trying to break free. Tilly stared down the corridor to see if anyone else had heard the commotion, but there was nobody about.

She gulped and took a deep breath.

It was an intimidating sight – a horse as powerful as that, rearing and smashing his hooves against the walls. He was a brown stallion, about 17hh, with a well-groomed, almost bronze sheen to his coat. It shimmered as he moved, like a sheet of velvet. He was obviously a very strong animal.

"Hello, boy!" she said softly, trying to catch his attention. If she could distract him, it might help to calm him down. She stared at a label that was attached to the door. It said 'Samson' in typed letters, and underneath that: 'Beware'.

78

"Hello there, Samson. I'm Tilly. What's the matter with you? I might be able to help. What's up?"

The horse stopped thrashing. He didn't look at Tilly, but she could tell that he was aware of her. She remembered how Magic Spirit had gradually responded to her attention, becoming more and more confident around her, once he was sure she was a friend.

She took hold of her horsehair bracelet and felt Magic's tail hairs between her fingers. Was he okay? she wondered. She had been so excited by everything that was happening at Olympia, she hadn't had the chance to worry about him. Suddenly it all came flooding back.

"Please be okay when I get home," she whispered. "Please be better."

The horse in the stall became completely still. He pricked up his ears. It seemed he was listening to her. Maybe he felt sorry for Magic Spirit too.

Instinctively, Tilly undid the bolt that

secured the door. She crept inside and reached her hand out. Slowly, the horse came to her. He leaned his nose towards her outstretched hand and began to explore it, nibbling and sniffing and getting used to her smell. His breath warmed her skin.

"That's it, Samson. Good boy. That's better. Take your time."

Samson gave a small snort and lifted his head. His face, which had been ferocious, was now relaxed. It was as if he was entranced. Tilly watched as the muscle tension in his body completely disappeared.

She stood beside him, and as she stroked his shoulders and back, she told him all about Magic Spirit – what a wonderful horse he was and how she hoped that he would make a full recovery from his colic. Samson listened patiently, rubbing his nose against Tilly's neck, and even letting her take some hair from his tail. I'll make a bracelet later, she thought. Soon, they had lost all track of time and were

responding to each other as though they
were the oldest of friends.

"What do you think you're doing?"

A sharp voice interrupted them.

Panicking, Tilly turned to see a young
man coming towards her. He went to take
hold of her arm and pull her out of the
stable, but when he saw what was
happening he stopped.

"Who are you?" he demanded.

"I-I'm Tilly Redbrow," she replied nervously.

"What are you doing in here? This isn't a public area!"

The man manoeuvred her out of the way and took hold of Samson's head collar. He looked him over as if he was checking for damage.

"I-I didn't hurt him," said Tilly. "I was trying to help ... I ... he ... I mean, he was getting distressed. I calmed him down."

"He gets like that," said the man gruffly, patting Samson's neck. "But you're lucky he didn't hurt you! He's a very temperamental horse. I'm his groom. I've seen some of the injuries he's given his handlers over the years. I don't know why his rider keeps going with him. He has so much ability but his brain always lets him down."

"Is he a Show Jumper?" asked Tilly.
"He's got the right conformation."

"Know a bit about horses, do you? He's
in the Puissance. He's definitely got a wild
side to him. He's capable of jumping higher
than any other horse, but I'm sure he'll let
us down again. Anyway, you still haven't
explained yourself. Do you make a habit
of entering the stalls of distressed horses?
It's extremely dangerous, you know."

Tilly couldn't decide how to explain it.

"I just ... do what I think is right," she
shrugged. "I don't know why but horses
seem to get on with me. People tell me
I've got a 'gift'."

She wasn't sure if the man believed her
or not. He stared at her for a moment, then
looked back at Samson, who was now
entirely placid. Eventually, he smiled.

"I've never seen him so settled. Usually
if he has one of his tempers, it takes several
people to get him calm and safe again.
Whatever you did, it's worked. What
exactly *did* you do?"

84

"I told him a story," said Tilly casually. "About a friend of mine."

The man looked puzzled for a moment, then he reached out his hand and took hold of Tilly's. He shook it in a grown up way.

"Thank you, Tilly Redbrow. I don't approve of you going into the stall of an upset horse unsupervised, but I appreciate your help. So does Samson. If you really do have a gift, then it's something very special. I'll tell Samson's owner about you. He might want to meet you. Where are you supposed to be now?"

"I'm with the—"

Tilly was about to finish her sentence, when the sound of footsteps and concerned voices filled the corridor. Will, plus Tilly's mum and several Olympia officials, were marching towards her. Tilly's mum broke into a run, her arms outstretched.

"They said they'd lost you!" she shrieked. "I was so worried! Where *have* you been?"

Tilly and the groom glanced at each other. They both smiled in a way that said 'Oh boy! Here we go!'. And then seconds later, Tilly was smothered by her mum's kisses and cuddles.

Nine

Tilly tried to explain to her mum and the officials that she had been distracted by the noise coming from Samson's stall, and then when she'd looked back, the tour party had gone. She wasn't sure whether to say anything about actually going into the stall and calming Samson down, but in the end the choice was made for her.

Not long after the officials turned up, two men appeared. One was older, wearing a smart suit, polished shoes and a long

brown winter coat. The younger one was
dressed in a red riding jacket and white
breeches. He was wearing immaculate
black leather riding boots. Tilly knew
instantly that he must be one of the
competitors in the show. When both men
started talking to the groom, Tilly also
realised they had something to do with
Samson.

"I heard there were problems again,"
said the older man. "One of the stable
hands said he's been making a commotion
on and off since lunchtime."

"He has," said the groom, "but it's
sorted now."

The younger man peered over the stall
door, and observed Samson's calm manner.
He turned back to the old man and
nodded. They both looked impressed.

"What 'appened?" he asked, in a
French accent.

"You'd better ask this girl," said the
groom, clamping his hands on Tilly's
shoulders.

Everyone looked at her. Her cheeks turned the colour of ripe tomatoes. She didn't know what to say.

"Go on," urged the groom. "This is your moment, Tilly Redbrow. Tell them how you managed to soothe Samson's temper."

"I," she began nervously, ". . . I went into his stall and . . ."

She looked at the anxious frown on her mum's face.

"I talked to him and stroked his neck, and eventually he seemed to settle. That's it really. I do it with lots of horses."

"Zat's it?" said the Frenchman. "Zat's all you did?"

Tilly nodded and gave a little smile.

"Well, as long as he's ready for the Puissance, zat's good enough for me. Thank you, young lady. Maybe now we'll win!"

"I had better tack him up now, Jean-Paul. We'll be called in a minute," said the groom.

"Wait! Before you go . . . " said Tilly. She turned away from the group and

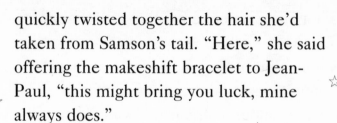

quickly twisted together the hair she'd taken from Samson's tail. "Here," she said offering the makeshift bracelet to Jean-Paul, "this might bring you luck, mine always does."

The rider looked surprised, but Tilly was pleased to see that he put it on.

"Thanks again, Tilly," the groom added as they turned to leave. "Jean-Paul and Samson are eighth to jump in the Puissance. Make sure you're watching."

Tilly looked at her mum. "We'd better get back to our seats," she said.

"Of course – let's go," said her mum in a daze. "Honestly, Tilly, the things you get yourself into. I can't keep up."

As they were walking away, the older man touched Tilly's arm. He handed her a small rectangular card.

"Before you go, Miss, my name's Arthur Hampton. I'm Samson's owner. That card's

got all my contact details on it. If you ever want to work with horses – perhaps when you're a bit older – give me a ring. Maybe I could do something for you. If I could bottle a talent like yours, I'd be laughing!"

Tilly took the card.

"Cool!" she said, with a twinkle in her eye. Well, it wasn't every day she got to visit Olympia, win a backstage tour, calm a distressed horse *and* get offered a dream job! Her mum squeezed her shoulder then they walked off down the corridor together.

"We haven't missed Father Christmas, have we?" she asked, although it felt to her as if Father Christmas had already been.

Mia and her mum waved them back to their seats.

"Quick!" said Mia. "It's about to start."

There were only three jumps in the ring. The first was a vertical, which Tilly thought must be a warm-up fence. The

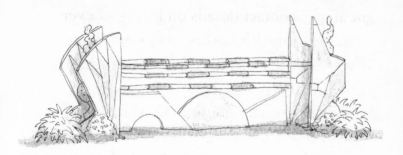

second was a big triple bar, and third came
a daunting bright-red brick wall, which
looked enormous and must have stood at
least six feet tall. And that was just the first
round!

"The wall goes up and up in each
round, and the horse that can jump the
highest wins," explained Mia.

"That'll be Samson," said Tilly
confidently.

"Who?"

Tilly told Mia the saga of her backstage
adventure. Mia shook her head and
laughed. "That could only happen to you,
Tilly. Look, here they go!"

The girls glued their gaze to the arena.
The entire place fell silent. One by one,

the horses came out and tackled the huge
walls. Tilly recognised Samson and Jean-
Paul instantly. They cleared everything,
along with some of the other horses.

In the first round, ten out of the fifteen
horses jumped clear. Then the wall went
up, and in the next round five more horses
were knocked out. In the third round, only
one went out. The other four horses,
Samson included, jumped the wall
superbly.

For the fourth round, the wall was massive. Tilly couldn't imagine *any* of the horses jumping it. The first two both clipped the top of the wall and the bricks came tumbling down. Then it was Samson's turn and, with fingers crossed, Tilly edged forward on her seat, willing him to clear it. The atmosphere bristled with tension.

"Imagine trying to get Rosie over that!" whispered Mia. "She'd have no hope!"

"Come on, Samson," Tilly whispered, as he cantered into the ring. "You can do it!"

As Samson calmly approached the wall, Tilly was amazed to see how slowly he was cantering. Surely he was never going to make it! But then Tilly couldn't believe the way he left the floor; it was almost as though he was on a spring board. He moved like rippling water, graceful and rhythmic, flying through the air, and clearing the wall with ease. Even before Samson had landed the audience erupted into applause.

Tilly sighed with relief. It was nerve-wracking stuff.

When the final horse came in, Tilly desperately hoped he would knock a brick out, so that victory would be Samson's – but he, like Samson, was successful.

Then, it was on to the fifth round, and now the wall now stood seven feet, four inches high.

Tilly and Mia looked at each other incredulously. They didn't think it was possible for *either* horse left in the competition to jump it.

"You'd have to have nerves of steel to even attempt *that*!" gulped Mia.

Samson entered the arena, and the crowd went quiet. Tilly twiddled with her horse hair bracelets, her eyes squeezed shut not daring to watch. She tried to picture as many happy things as she could – riding lessons with Rosie, Magic Spirit getting better, owning her own stables, helping top horses with her whispering skills.

It was only when she heard the screams
and cheers of appreciation from the crowd
that she knew Samson had cleared the wall.

As the last horse came into the ring,
silence descended once more. Again Tilly
didn't dare watch; just hoped and hoped
that Samson would be the winner. She
opened her eyes as she heard the audience
gasp – the final horse had refused at the
wall, and the rider was holding up his hand
to signal retirement.

Samson had won the Puissance!

Tilly and Mia jumped to their feet as
the audience burst into rapturous applause.

"Remarkable!" yelled the commentator.

Jean-Paul leaned forward to
congratulate Samson, then threw his hat
into the air. Tilly noticed with pride that
he was still wearing the bracelet she had
made for him. Then she saw Jean-Paul
look about the audience and mouthed
the word *merci*!

Tilly recognised it as the French word
for 'thank you'.

98

And maybe, she thought, just maybe, he'd intended it for her.

Ten

After the Puissance, the arena was prepared for the Grand Finale. Soon the sound of bagpipes began to fill the air, and the girls knew it was about to start. This was one of the performances they had looked forward to the most.

Hundreds of pipers wearing tartan kilts marched in, surrounded by smoke and spotlights. They were followed by a troop of soldiers on horseback, who performed a series of dressage movements in perfect synchrony.

"There are so many of them," said Tilly, "and they're all doing exactly the same thing. Those horses must be well trained."

"If Rosie was there she'd be, like, stepping out of line and trying to chew the other horse's tails and stuff!"

The girls giggled.

The pipers began to play 'Hark the Herald Angels Sing' and the audience clapped and sang along. Mia's mum passed round a box of mince pies, to add to the festivity.

"I feel really Christmassy now," said Mia.

"Look!" gasped Tilly, pointing to the ceiling of the arena.

Hundreds of tiny snowflakes were falling over them.

"How's that happening?" wondered Mia, confused.

"They're not real," said Tilly, catching one in her hand. "They're made of paper."

"I wouldn't like to be the one who tidies them all up," said Tilly's mum, shaking her head.

Soon the whole arena was filled with tiny flecks of white. It was like being inside a snow globe, and with the effect of the dry-ice smoke, it looked really magical. A faint sound of sleigh bells signalled the arrival of Father Christmas, and suddenly, there he was on a magnificent horse-drawn sleigh. He waved at the audience and got them to sing 'Jingle Bells'. When it finished everyone cheered like mad.

It was a fantastic end to a wonderful show.

"Time to go," said Tilly's mum.

"We'll have to come again next year," said Mia.

"Definitely," said Tilly, wondering if she might ever come to the show as a performer, with Magic Spirit perhaps.

As a treat, the girls got to have dinner in the local pizzeria, and then they watched highlights from the Olympia show on the television in the hotel lobby.

"I can't believe we were actually there!" said Tilly. "It's like a dream!"

It was particularly exciting to watch the replay of Samson and Jean-Paul's triumph in the Puissance. The wall looked even higher through the lens of the television camera. Tilly was pleased she had played a part in that success. She made sure she put Arthur Hampton's card in a safe place, inside her purse.

All in all, it had been a very enjoyable trip. Although Tilly was sad that it was over, she couldn't wait to get back to see Magic Spirit and tell him all her news. As the coach pulled away from London next morning her thoughts turned to him.

She talked about nothing else for the whole
journey, so in the end, her mum agreed that
as soon as the coach dropped them off and
their bags were unpacked, she would give
Tilly a lift to Silver Shoe Farm.

By the time they actually got back, it
was four o'clock. The sky was dark and
starry and the yard was quiet. Tilly raced
over to Magic Spirit's stable but it was
empty. Although she knew there was
probably a sensible explanation for this,
her stomach was full of butterflies.

"We've got to find him," she urged,
pulling her mum towards the long field. A
few horses were huddling together, wearing
warm blankets, but there was no Magic
Spirit.

Next, they checked the outdoor arena.
Although the floodlights were on, there was
nobody there either.

"Where is he?" she whispered under
her breath.

Even Tilly's mum was starting to worry
now. Luckily they spotted Duncan darting

105

towards the indoor school. They ran after him.

"Hey, guys!" he said. "How was your trip?"

"It was great," said Tilly hastily. "But where's Magic? You haven't had to have him put down have you?" she pleaded, almost tearful.

Duncan shook his head.

"Quite the opposite," he smiled. "Come with me."

He led them into the brightly-lit indoor school, and there, in the middle, was Magic Spirit, fully tacked up with Angela sitting on his back. She waved when she saw Tilly and her mum, but for Tilly there was no time to wave back. She ran towards Magic and threw her arms around him. It was a relief and a joy to see him again. And he seemed delighted to see her. His ears pricked up and he nuzzled her neck and shoulders.

Tilly thought he looked more magnificent than ever. He held his head

106

high and everything about him suggested speed and power. After the difficulties he'd been through, Tilly knew he was fighter. Like her, he was determined to do his best, and she was certain that one day he'd prove himself in competition.

"He's on great form," said Angela. "The vet gave him the all-clear yesterday. We've been exercising him this afternoon and he seems very settled. We're trying to prepare him."

"We reckon he'll be ready for you to have your first ride soon, maybe after the New Year."

Mrs Redbrow put her arm around her daughter.

"All that worrying, eh? There you go – that's the best news you could hope for."

Tilly's heart fluttered. Of all the exciting things that had happened, and of all the Christmas presents she was going to get this year, she already knew what her favourite one was. The promise of her first ride on Magic Spirit couldn't be beaten.

She tickled his shoulder, and in response, he turned around and nudged her gently with his nose.

"Merry Christmas, Magic!" she whispered. "You're the best!"

109

Pippa's Top Tips

When you're learning to jump, remember it's not about how high you can go, but about perfecting the basics to boost both yours and your pony's confidence.

Jumping exercises over poles and cross poles will help you learn to judge your stride, to maintain rhythm and teach you to sit straight.

Balance is one of the most important things to remember when you're learning to jump. Forgetting about balance on take-off is one of the main reasons riders fall off!

Before tackling a jump, top show jumpers always walk the course to get a sense of the distance. Try it yourself.

Four of your strides is about equal to one horse stride. Allow two of your strides for the distance from the fence to where your pony is going to land, and two more in front of the next fence for where he'll take off.

Try to meet the jump on an even stride. Your pony shouldn't have to suddenly take a great long stride before the cross poles or a very short one.

Don't worry if you don't get it right first time! Learning to jump takes determination and practice, but you'll get there in the end.

'Aids' is a term used for the parts of the body which give commands or signals to horses when riding them.

Use your leg to change pace – move forward with a nudge, or close your leg for a downward transition. Use your hand for direction and control.

Your seat and back will help balance your pony; this will also help enormously with control and changing pace. You can also use your voice as an aid.

For more about Tilly and Silver Shoe Farm –
including pony tips, quizzes and everything
you ever wanted to know about horses – visit
www.tillysponytails.co.uk